This Little Tiger book belongs to:

Ethane

To my family
~NG

To Paul, with thanks
~MT

LITTLE TIGER PRESS
An imprint of Magi Publications
1 The Coda Centre, 189 Munster Road, London SW6 6AW
www.littletigerpress.com

First published in Great Britain 2004
This edition published 2005
Text copyright © Nicola Grant 2004
Illustrations copyright © Michael Terry 2004
Nicola Grant and Michael Terry have asserted their rights
to be identified as the author and illustrator of this work
under the Copyright, Designs and Patents Act, 1988
All rights reserved • ISBN 1 84506 015 6
A CIP catalogue record for this book is available
from the British Library
Printed in China
10 9 8 7 6 5 4 3 2 1

Chameleon's Crazy Colours

By Nicola Grant *and* Michael Terry

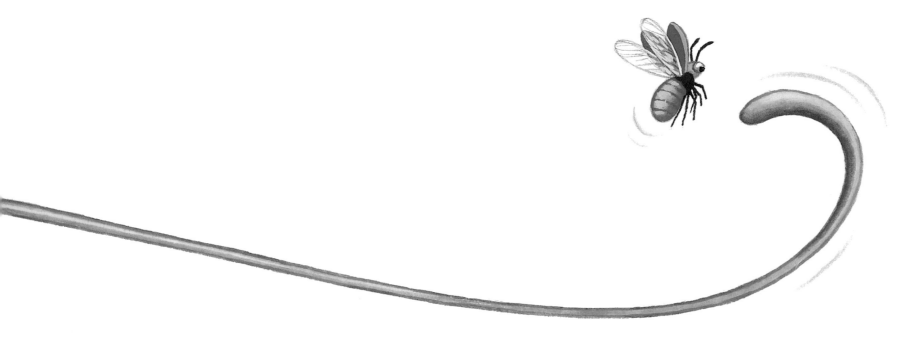

Little Tiger Press

London

Deep in the rainforest all was not well. Chameleon was having trouble with his colours.

"Bother!" he said crossly. "I'm sitting on yellow flowers so I should be yellow. But look at me – I'm red!"

Chameleon hopped on to a stone,
and turned blue with pink spots.

Walking through the grass,
he went orange!
It was all horribly wrong!

Monkey and Meercat strolled by. "You look a bit off-colour today!" they said.

"I'm in a colour muddle!" Chameleon cried. "I knew I shouldn't have eaten that funny-looking bug last night! What if Lion comes prowling? If I can't change colour he'll see me and eat me up!"

"Easy!" said Monkey. "We'll help!"

"No problem!" said Meercat.

"Close your eyes and *think* yourself a colour!" said Meercat.

"I am yellow, I am yellow," chanted Chameleon. He started pacing up and down. But . . .

"WHOOAAHH!"

Chameleon slipped on Monkey's old banana skin and skidded into a mango tree!

SPLAT! A big ripe mango fell on his head!

"Ouch! I *am* yellow now!" said Chameleon crossly.

"Well *that* didn't work! I need another plan."

"Easy!" said Monkey.

"No problem!" said Meercat.

Later, as Chameleon lay deep in thought on his favourite branch, two figures tiptoed up . . .

"Lion is coming!" they shouted. "It's LION!"

"Aaargh!" Chameleon tried to turn green –
but went purple!
He leapt towards some purple flowers
to hide . . .

SPLASH!
Chameleon fell into the river!
Coughing and spluttering, he
scrambled aboard a floating log.
  "Only joking!" shouted Monkey and
Meercat. "We thought if we gave you a
scare your colours would work properly."

That night Monkey and Meercat met in secret
to make more plans.

"What a brilliant idea!" Monkey whispered.
"Let's do it!"

By dawn, the pair were ready for action.
   "This disguise is *really* scary!" Meercat
said. "The fright will definitely make
Chameleon's wonky colours work!"
   "Stand by!" hushed Monkey.
"Chameleon's coming!"

"GRRRRR!"

   With a great rumbling roar Monkey leapt out.

   "Help, it's LION!" Chameleon gasped. He tried to turn green – but went red!

   "Only me!" laughed Monkey. "Just trying to help again!"

   "Great disguise," said Chameleon. "Shame it didn't work!"

But Monkey and Meercat wouldn't give up.

"LION!" they shouted as Chameleon munched his crunchy lunch.

Chameleon almost choked on his beetle. Instead of going brown, he went blue!

"LION!" screeched Meercat as Chameleon slurped a drink. Chameleon hid amongst some pink flowers. But everyone saw him – he was bright orange!

"It's hopeless!" Chameleon sighed.

"Hmm. Not so easy," said Monkey.

"Bit of a problem!" said Meercat.

Chameleon flopped into the shade, feeling terribly worried. Nothing worked! What would he do if Lion *really* came?

Just then, Meercat and Monkey shot past. They looked scared. Very scared.

"Lion!" they squeaked.

"Ha, ha! You don't fool me!" Chameleon laughed. But just then he heard a very loud GRRRRRR!

Chameleon froze. He looked up and gulped a big gulp. "GULP!"

Lion was towering over him!

"What are you?" said Lion, licking his lips.

"I-I-I'm a red spotted thingy," Chameleon stuttered. "No, I'm pink and purple. Erm, now I'm red and blue *and* purple!"

Lion looked puzzled. Suddenly Chameleon had a brainwave!

"I've got Funny-Colouritis!"
Chameleon told Lion.
"Swallow me and you'll
get an icky tummy!"
   "Funny-Colouritis?"
growled Lion, backing away
fast. "Are you sure?"
   "Oh, yes!" Chameleon said.
"Eat me and you'll end up
looking crazy coloured like
me, too!"

"Yikes!" gasped Lion,
quaking with fear. "I'm off!"
   And he disappeared in a
cloud of dust.

"Three cheers for clever Chameleon!" laughed Monkey. "He's got rid of that Lion for ever!"

"Hooray for Chameleon's funny colours!" Meercat cried.

And Chameleon was so happy he went pink with pleasure – with bright blue and orange spots, of course!

More crazy capers from Little Tiger Press

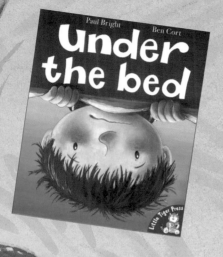

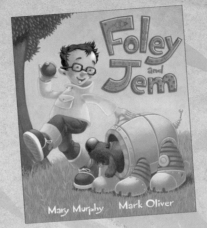

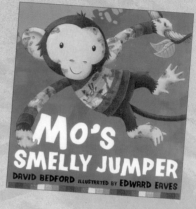

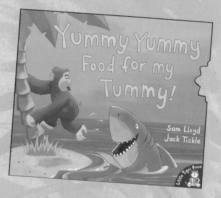

For information regarding any of the above titles
or for our catalogue, please contact us:
Little Tiger Press, 1 The Coda Centre,
189 Munster Road, London SW6 6AW
Tel: 020 7385 6333 Fax: 020 7385 7333
Email: info@littletiger.co.uk
www.littletigerpress.com